THE BIRD THAT FLEW WITH ONE WING

PAULY THE PEREGRINE

Teach your kids to pray;
The Lord's Prayer included

AMINA A. AZIZ

Balboa Press books may be ordered through booksellers or by contacting:

Balboa Press
A Division of Hay House
1663 Liberty Drive
Bloomington, IN 47403
www.balboapress.com
844-682-1282

Because of the dynamic nature of the Internet, any web addresses or links contained in this book may have changed since publication and may no longer be valid. The views expressed in this work are solely those of the author and do not necessarily reflect the views of the publisher, and the publisher hereby disclaims any responsibility for them.

Any people depicted in stock imagery provided by Getty Images are models, and such images are being used for illustrative purposes only. Certain stock imagery © Getty Images.

Scripture quotations marked KJV are from the Holy Bible, King James Version (Authorized Version). First published in 1611. Quoted from the KJV Classic Reference Bible, Copyright © 1983 by The Zondervan Corporation.

ISBN: 978-1-9822-7304-0 (sc)
ISBN: 978-1-9822-7305-7 (e)

Library of Congress Control Number: 2021916440

Print information available on the last page.

Balboa Press rev. date: 08/13/2021

BALBOA.PRESS
A DIVISION OF HAY HOUSE

Dedication

Thank you Most High for giving me the spirit of
endurance and the strength to chase my dreams.
To my children and grandchildren, Aleuah, Antonius, Aisha,
Akil, A'Micael, Stephen, Rodriquez, Layla, Dae'Sean, Amir and
Zymir everything I do and have ever done is for you all, I am so
grateful I was chosen to be you all's mother and grandmother.
To my daddy thank you for always telling me I was a princess
and for never letting anyone hurt me. I miss you every day.
To my momma Baseemah, my sisters Khadijah
and Halimah I love you all always.
To my nephews Muneer, Aquantus,
Dominique, Hasan, and baby Floyd.
To my nieces Hajah and Jania, I love you all.
To my aunts Sandra Martin and Cynthia Atkins.
To my grandmother Annie Rainey.
To my cousins Jeff Martin, Messiah, and Raphael.
And to my dear friends William, Charonda,
and Sheree, I love you all.

The hardest thing to be in life is someone other than yourself-
Amina

It was a beautiful sunny fall day in Cape Code, Massachusetts. In an old Pitch Pine tree near the very top there was a family of Peregrine Falcons. The Peregrines were cozy and comfortable in their nest. Maggie, the momma bird was sitting patiently watching her egg waiting on it to hatch. Charlie the poppa bird was out gathering food. There was a soft crackling sound as Maggie exclaimed,

"It's coming! It's coming!"

As Charlie flew in the nest a tiny baby Peregrine was emerging from its shell. Out came a male Peregrine bird slimy and flapping. As Maggie coddled her baby Charlie shouted,

"He has one wing!"

Charlie reminded Maggie that through Christ anything is possible to him who believes. Faith is believing in the unbelievable. God will make miracles happen to all who believe in His Word. Charlie reminded Maggie that in the bible *Psalm 34:19 says "many are the afflictions of the righteous but the Lord delivereth him out of them all"* (KJV)

Charlie and Maggie hugged one another and cried,

"What will we name him?"

Maggie gently whispered to Charlie. "I know." Maggie cried out

"Pauly!"

With so much love Maggie and Charlie hugged and welcomed their baby bird Pauly, into the world.

"He is special. He only has one wing."

Charlie mentioned. Maggie looked at her baby Peregrine and said,

"Pauly you are the same as all the other Peregrines, you have one wing I am sure you will be able to fly! Because the word of God teaches us through Christ all things are possible to him who believes by faith anything is possible."

As the days grew on, Pauly got bigger and was so beautiful he had a touch of black on the tip of his beech, with long beautiful brown feathers but Pauly only had one wing. Pauly's mom flew him to the ground. The beautiful young Peregrine looked at his mother with his big black eyes and asked,

"Why do I only have one wing momma?"

Maggie responded with kindness, "God created you so the other Peregrines could see a miracle!"

Pauly was out the nest playing one day on the ground. He met the other Peregrine birds from his tree for the first time. Pauly was so happy and excited! There was Don, Layla, Steve and Mike. All the young Peregrines ran and flew around playing below the tree. Pauly watched them wishing he could fly! He put his head down and started crying! Layla looked at him and said don't leave Pauly! I will stay here and play with you! Pauly, turned around and hugged Layla. They talked on the branch while the other birds played beneath them.

The young Peregrines kicked the acorns around and laughed. Pauly looked at Layla and said,

"One day I will fly with just one wing. My mother told me I am a miracle and through Christ anything is possible even flying with one wing."

Layla looked confused, and asked Pauly,

"Who is Christ?"

"He is the only begotten Son of God. He died on the cross for the sins of the whole world; He is the example we should follow on how to treat one another." Pauly responded

"Wow!" Layla responded. "I want to follow his example."

"You are! You have a good heart that is why you play with me and don't treat me differently because I have one wing. My momma told me God created us perfectly in His image and He does not make mistakes." Pauly, responded.

They both went to their nests that night feeling peace and love.

The next day Steve, Don and Mike went to Pauly's nest. Maggie said,

"Good morning, kids. How are you guys doing?"

"Fine!" They all exclaimed together.

"Can Pauly come out and play with us? Please!"

"He sure can." said Maggie.

"Pauly do you want to kick the acorn with us?"

"Yes, I do! Where is Layla?"

"Layla is not feeling well", said Steve.

"What is wrong with her?" replied Don.

"Nothing serious! She is just not feeling well today. She has a cold, maybe we should pray for her."

"I've never prayed before", said the other Peregrines.

"My mother said praying is just like talking to your best friend", Pauly stated. "God is the friend who can change anything and make it better."

All the Peregrines held up their wings together as Pauly instructed and simply said, "Please God, heal Layla from her cold and make her better." They exclaimed together.

So Be It! Prayer is not just about going to God in need of people, places and things. The biggest prayer is just to go to God in gratitude. God loves thankfulness.

The Lord's Prayer
Matthew 6: 9-13 (KJV)

Our Father, who art in heaven hollowed be Thy name,
Thy kingdom come thy will be done on earth as it is in heaven.
Give us this day our daily bread
and forgive us our trespasses
as we forgive those who trespass against us
and lead us not into temptation
but deliver us from evil.
For thine is the kingdom and the power
and the glory for ever and ever.
Amen.

As the young Peregrines went to Layla's nest to see how she was doing. They were all overjoyed to see that she was feeling much better.

"Layla!" Mike said.

"Are you coming out to play with us?"

"Yes!" She said.

Layla ran and gave all the young Peregrines a hug.

All the young Peregrines said

"Let's fly down!"

Don shouted "Pauly! Fly!"

Pauly ran and flapped his strong beautiful wing and behold the miracle of God. Pauly flew and flew and soared across the beautiful sky. Maggie and Charlie came out of their nest and watched Pauly soar across the beautiful trees. Maggie smiled at Charlie and said,

"Behold, the miracle of God!"

Pauly is the bird that flew with one wing.

THE END

About Amina A. Aziz

Amina, is an exciting future New York Times Best Selling children's book author bringing valuable life lessons and spirituality together for individuals of all ages to enjoy. Amina has dedicated her life to motivating and empowering humanity. She is a philanthropist and a dedicated and loving mother and grandmother who loves all of creation. Amina enjoys traveling, reading, writing and art of all genres. She brings an upbeat heartwarming colorful and friendly take on combining nature and human spirit of compassion together to bring you a compassionate heartwarming literary experience.

Color Your Own

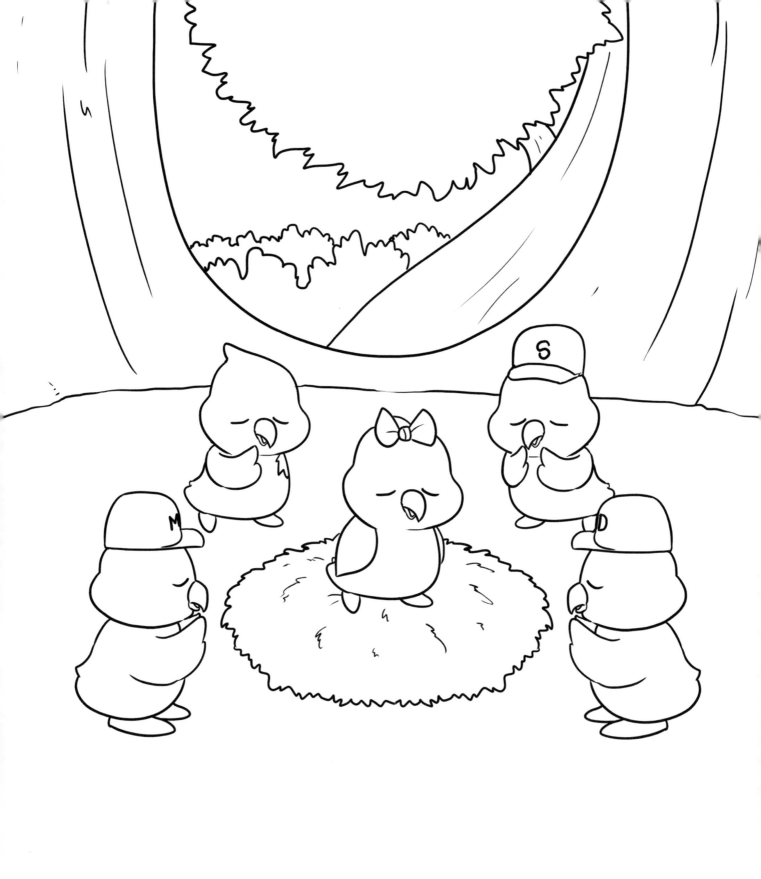

Printed in the United States
by Baker & Taylor Publisher Services